To

....

From

....

Dedication

To my husband, Timothy,

the man who romanced me off my feet and

set my heart a' poundin'.

Romantic

TO SHOW THE LOVE YOU FEEL

NOTIONS

Lisa Tawn Bergren

MULTNOMAH BOOKS

ROMANTIC NOTIONS
published by Multnomah Books
a part of the Questar publishing family

© 1993 by Lisa Tawn Bergren

Illustrations by Cyd Moore

Edited by Shari MacDonald

International Standard Book Number 0-88070-652-X

Printed in the United States of America

Scripture quotations are from the New International Version
© 1973, 1984 by International Bible Society
used by permission of Zondervan Publishing House

Life's Little Instruction Book, H. Jackson Brown, Jr.
Rutledge Hill Press, © 1991 by H. Jackson Brown, Jr.

94 95 96 97 98 99 00 01 — 10 9 8 7 6 5 4 3 2

Doubt thou the stars are fire;
Doubt that the sun doth move;
Doubt truth to be a liar;
But never doubt I love.

–WILLIAM SHAKESPEARE

A Note from the Author

Once in a while, God gives a gift so precious, the person receiving it can only stand back in shock and wonder: *How could I be so blessed? Why has He chosen me?* The sweetest gift I've been given is the relationship I share with my husband, Timothy.

What is the best part of our marriage? Being best friends. When I was a child, I saw my own parents demonstrate that kind of friendship—and it has proven to be the greatest teaching on love they've ever given me.

As friends, Tim and I look forward to a lifetime of learning about and enjoying one another. A vital part of our marriage is romance, something that came easily in courting, but now needs to be carefully cultivated as "old married folks."

I believe that romance is something that women truly crave and men enjoy. It keeps things interesting, makes each of us more attractive, pushes us to remember why we chose each other in the first place...and brings our love *alive*.

*L*ook at your love with renewed vision. *It is God's gift.* Honor it. Setting the stage for romance is not always easy... but it is always worth it.

—LISA TAWN BERGREN

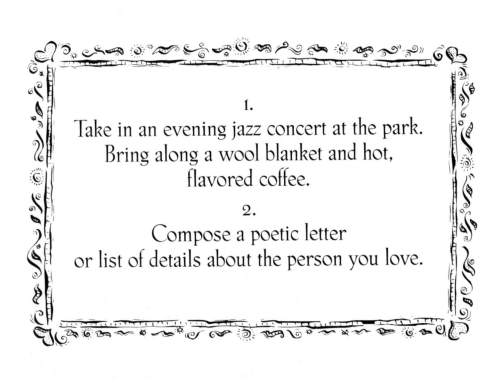

1.

Take in an evening jazz concert at the park.
Bring along a wool blanket and hot,
flavored coffee.

2.

Compose a poetic letter
or list of details about the person you love.

Slow dance.

—H. JACKSON BROWN, JR.
#80, *LIFE'S LITTLE INSTRUCTION BOOK*

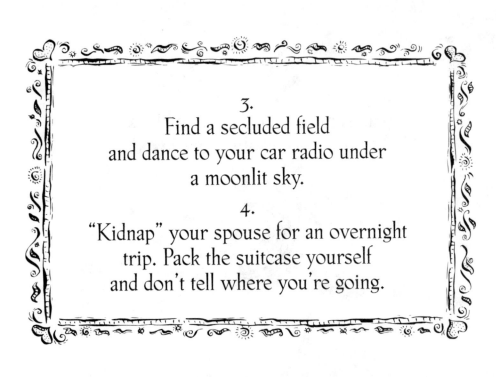

3.
Find a secluded field
and dance to your car radio under
a moonlit sky.

4.
"Kidnap" your spouse for an overnight
trip. Pack the suitcase yourself
and don't tell where you're going.

The supreme happiness of life is the conviction that we are loved.

—Victor Hugo

5.
Watch the moon rise
while cuddling under a blanket.

6.
Find an old chapel and
sing your favorite hymns together.

[Love] burns like a blazing fire,
like a mighty flame.
Many waters canot quench love;
rivers cannot wash it away.

–SONG OF SONGS 8:7

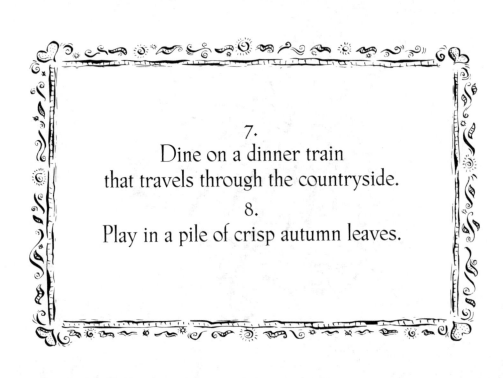

7.
Dine on a dinner train
that travels through the countryside.

8.
Play in a pile of crisp autumn leaves.

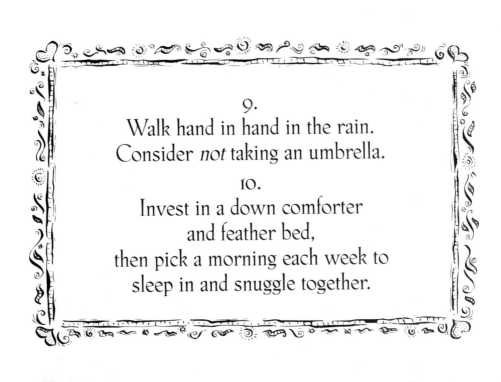

9.
Walk hand in hand in the rain.
Consider *not* taking an umbrella.

10.
Invest in a down comforter
and feather bed,
then pick a morning each week to
sleep in and snuggle together.

Let us not love with words or tongue
but with actions and in truth.

—I JOHN 3:18

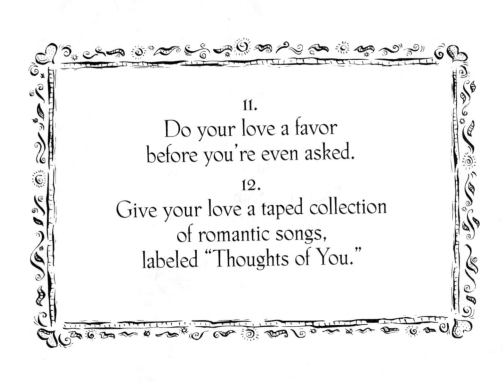

11.
Do your love a favor
before you're even asked.

12.
Give your love a taped collection
of romantic songs,
labeled "Thoughts of You."

My heart shall be
The faithful compass
That still points to thee.
—VERSE FROM A NINETEENTH-CENTURY CARD

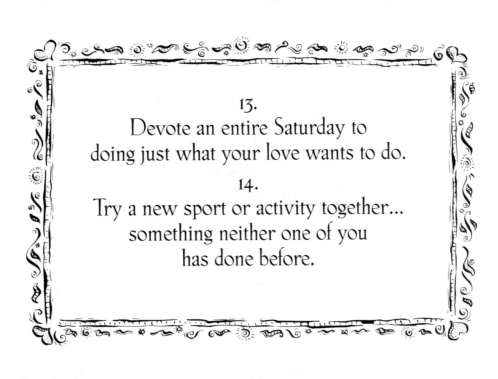

13.
Devote an entire Saturday to
doing just what your love wants to do.

14.
Try a new sport or activity together...
something neither one of you
has done before.

Everyone should be quick to listen,
slow to speak
and slow to become angry.

—JAMES 1:19B

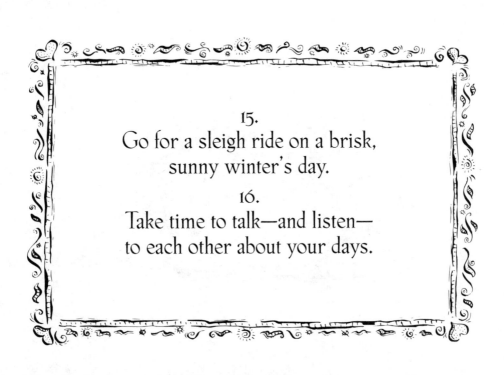

15.
Go for a sleigh ride on a brisk,
sunny winter's day.

16.
Take time to talk—and listen—
to each other about your days.

17.
Enjoy a picnic by the ocean.

18.
Explore new places together,
in your neighborhood...
and beyond.

Love is a fruit in season at all times,
and within the reach of every hand.

—MOTHER THERESA

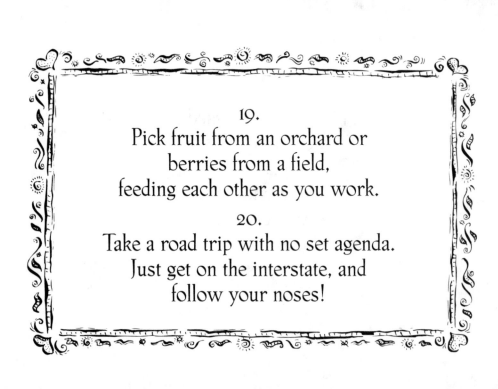

19.
Pick fruit from an orchard or
berries from a field,
feeding each other as you work.

20.
Take a road trip with no set agenda.
Just get on the interstate, and
follow your noses!

First time he kissed me,
he but only kissed
The fingers of this hand
where with I write;
And, ever since,
it grew more clean and white.

—Elizabeth Barrett Browning

21.
Plant a garden together,
including each person's three
favorite flowers.

22.
Sit knee to knee and whisper things
you love about each other.

As long as one can admire and love,
then one is young forever.

—Pablo Casals

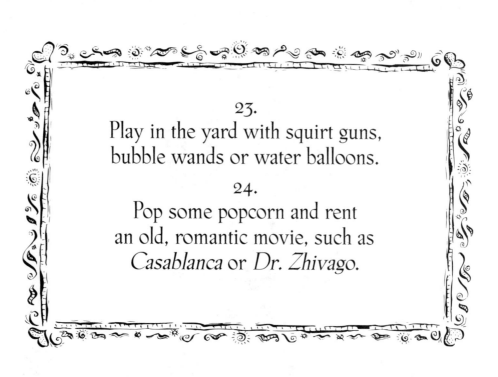

23.

Play in the yard with squirt guns,
bubble wands or water balloons.

24.

Pop some popcorn and rent
an old, romantic movie, such as
Casablanca or *Dr. Zhivago*.

25.
Surprise your love
with a huge bouquet of red roses.
Or just one.

26.
Read the morning paper together.
Start with the comics!

Talk not of wasted affection.
Affection never was wasted.

—LONGFELLOW

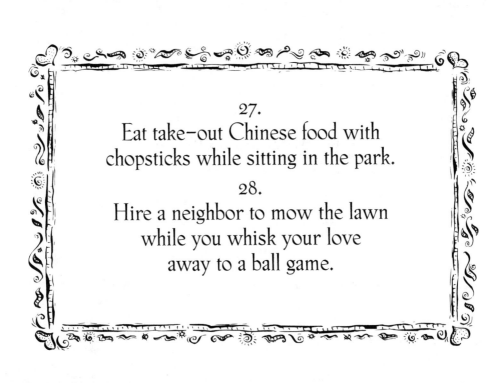

27.
Eat take-out Chinese food with
chopsticks while sitting in the park.

28.
Hire a neighbor to mow the lawn
while you whisk your love
away to a ball game.

Love is always worth the effort...

—LEO BUSCAGLIA, *BUS 9 TO PARADISE*

29.
Go out for a romantic dinner,
for no particular reason.

30.
Sit in an outdoor hot tub
under a starry sky.

You are always new.
The last of your kisses was
ever the sweetest;
the last smile the brightest;
the last movement the gracefullest.

—JOHN KEATS

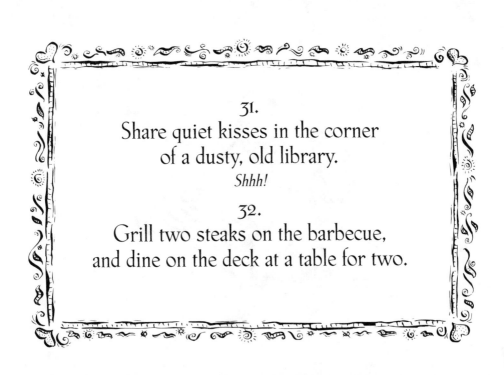

31.
Share quiet kisses in the corner
of a dusty, old library.
Shhh!

32.
Grill two steaks on the barbecue,
and dine on the deck at a table for two.

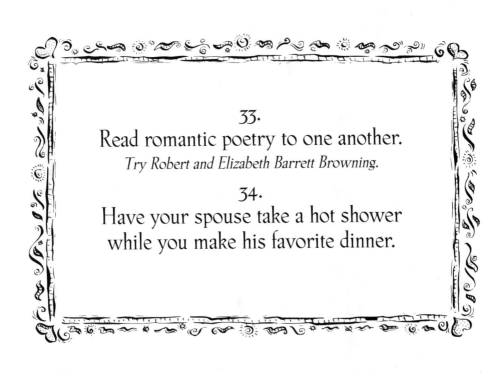

33.
Read romantic poetry to one another.
Try Robert and Elizabeth Barrett Browning.

34.
Have your spouse take a hot shower
while you make his favorite dinner.

Love is patient, love is kind.
It does not boast, it is not proud.
It is not rude, it is not self-seeking,
it is not easily angered,
it keeps no record of wrongs.

—I Corinthians 13:4-5

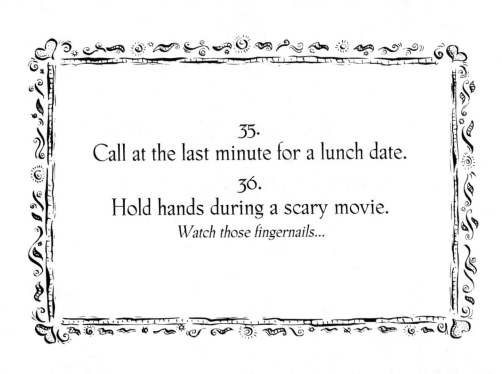

35.
Call at the last minute for a lunch date.

36.
Hold hands during a scary movie.
Watch those fingernails...

Love does not delight in evil
but rejoices in truth.
It always protects, always trusts,
always hopes, always perseveres.

—I CORINTHIANS 13:6–7

37.
Bundle up and search the woods together
for "the perfect Christmas tree."

38.
Sketch your dream house together.

And now these three remain:
faith, hope and love.
But the greatest of these is love.

—I CORINTHIANS 13:13

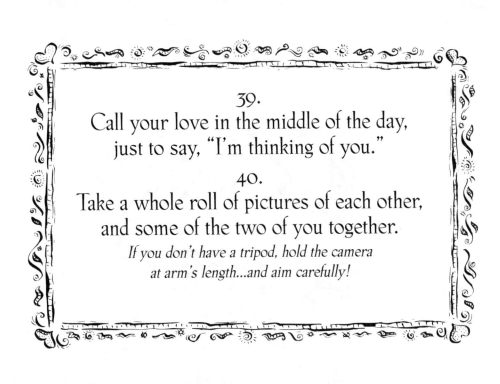

39.
Call your love in the middle of the day,
just to say, "I'm thinking of you."

40.
Take a whole roll of pictures of each other,
and some of the two of you together.
*If you don't have a tripod, hold the camera
at arm's length...and aim carefully!*

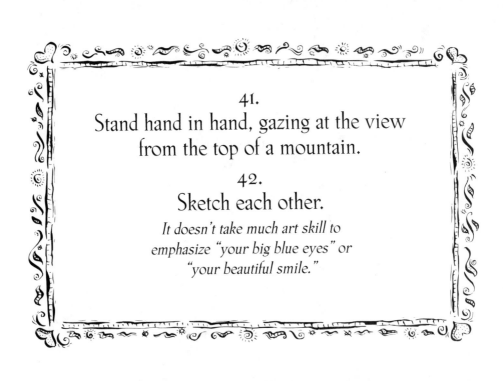

41.
Stand hand in hand, gazing at the view
from the top of a mountain.

42.
Sketch each other.

*It doesn't take much art skill to
emphasize "your big blue eyes" or
"your beautiful smile."*

Love never fails.

—I Corinthians 13:8

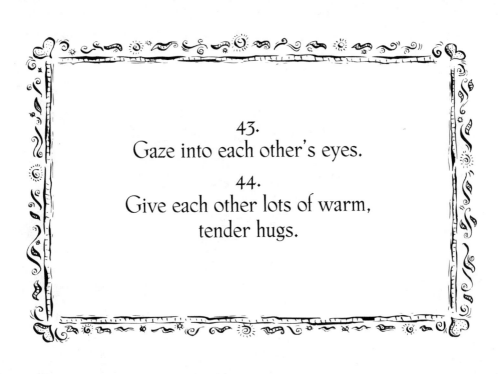

43.
Gaze into each other's eyes.

44.
Give each other lots of warm,
tender hugs.

One word Frees us
of all the weight and pain of life:
That word is love.

—SOPHOCLES

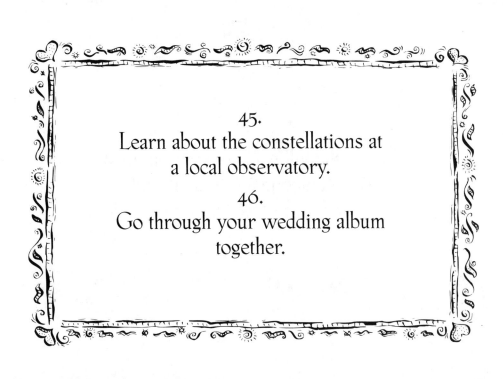

45.
Learn about the constellations at
a local observatory.

46.
Go through your wedding album
together.

To get the full value of joy you must
have someone to divide it with.

—MARK TWAIN

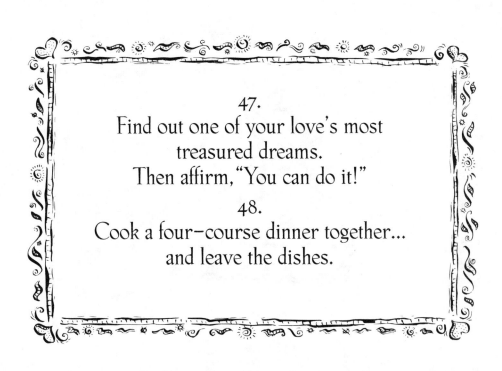

47.
Find out one of your love's most
treasured dreams.
Then affirm, "You can do it!"

48.
Cook a four-course dinner together...
and leave the dishes.

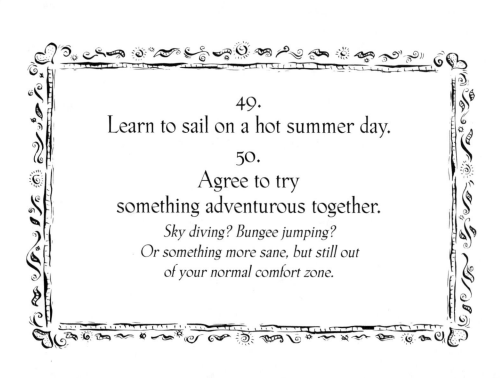

49.
Learn to sail on a hot summer day.

50.
Agree to try
something adventurous together.

*Sky diving? Bungee jumping?
Or something more sane, but still out
of your normal comfort zone.*

Familiar acts are beautiful through love.

—Percy Bysshe Shelley

51.
Cultivate good smells in the kitchen
and chat together while you cook.

52.
Turn on the answering machine
even when you're home.
*For an evening, don't talk to anyone
but each other.*

Come live with me, and be my love,
And we will some new pleasures prove,
Of golden sands, and crystal brooks,
With silken lines, and silver hooks.

—JOHN DONNE

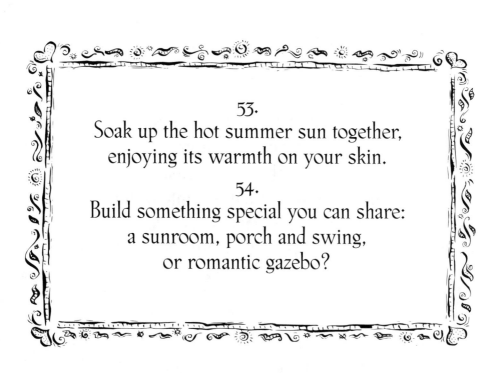

53.
Soak up the hot summer sun together,
enjoying its warmth on your skin.

54.
Build something special you can share:
a sunroom, porch and swing,
or romantic gazebo?

Love is a universal thirst
for a communion,
not merely of the senses,
but of our whole nature, intellectual,
imaginative and sensitive.

—BENJAMIN DISRAELI

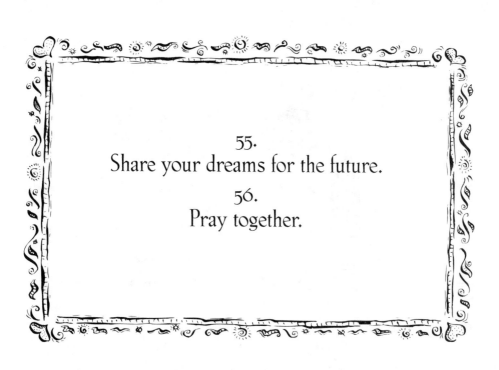

55.
Share your dreams for the future.

56.
Pray together.

57.
Hide love notes in unexpected places.

58.
Make "angels" in the snow,
and then warm up over mugs of
steaming hot chocolate.

To love and be loved
is the greatest happiness of existence.

—FROM JO PETTY'S
COMPILATION *WINGS OF SILVER*

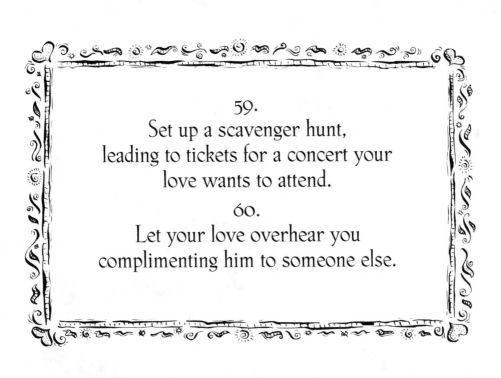

59.
Set up a scavenger hunt,
leading to tickets for a concert your
love wants to attend.

60.
Let your love overhear you
complimenting him to someone else.

Love is a deep well from
which you may drink often,
but into which you may fall but once.

—ELLYE HOWELL GLOVER

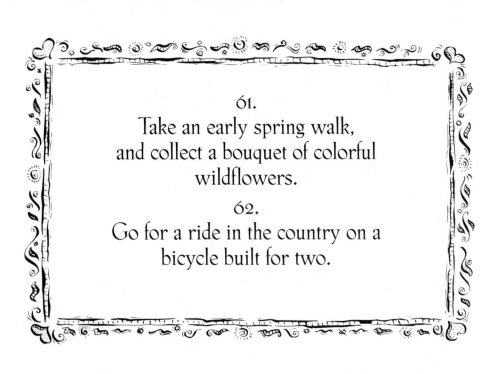

61.
Take an early spring walk,
and collect a bouquet of colorful
wildflowers.

62.
Go for a ride in the country on a
bicycle built for two.

The weather is fine
while people are courting...

—Robert Louis Stevenson

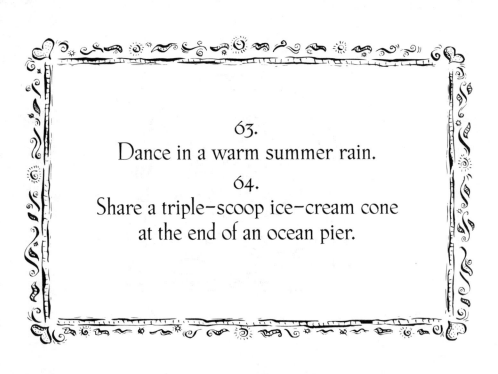

63.
Dance in a warm summer rain.

64.
Share a triple-scoop ice-cream cone
at the end of an ocean pier.

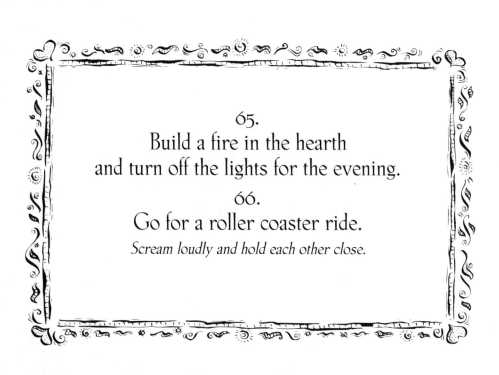

65.
Build a fire in the hearth
and turn off the lights for the evening.

66.
Go for a roller coaster ride.
Scream loudly and hold each other close.

My heart to you is given:
oh, do give yours to me:
We'll lock them up together,
and throw away the key.

—FREDERICK SAUNDERS, 1871

67.
Skate outdoors on a local frozen pond.
Remember safety—go only where authorized.

68.
Shout "I love you" into an echoing canyon:
"I LOVE YOU!...I LOVE YOU!...I LOVE YOU!"

Some people fall in love with the swiftness and force of an electric shock, while with others the process is so gradual that the fact is not discovered until some accident or emergency reveals it to the interior perception.

—JENNIE JUNE, 1864

69.
Read a classic love story together.
Check out Romeo and Juliet *or* Two from Galilee.

70.
Write love messages in the sand,
and hold each other close
as the waves wash them away.

But to see her was to love her,
Love but her, and love for ever.

—ROBERT BURNS

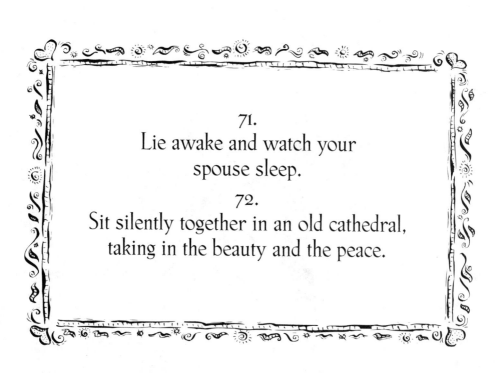

71.
Lie awake and watch your
spouse sleep.

72.
Sit silently together in an old cathedral,
taking in the beauty and the peace.

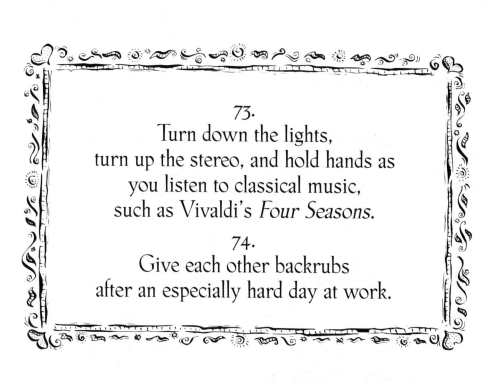

73.
Turn down the lights,
turn up the stereo, and hold hands as
you listen to classical music,
such as Vivaldi's *Four Seasons*.

74.
Give each other backrubs
after an especially hard day at work.

Respect for each other is as necessary
to a happy marriage
as that the husband and wife should
have an affection for one another.

—JOHN H. YOUNG, 1879

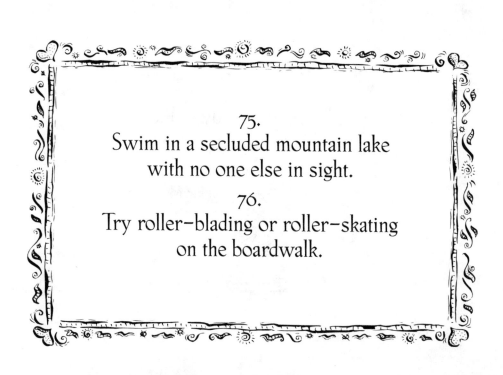

75.
Swim in a secluded mountain lake
with no one else in sight.

76.
Try roller-blading or roller-skating
on the boardwalk.

The great tragedy of life
is not that men perish,
but that they cease to love.

—W. SOMERSET MAUGHAM

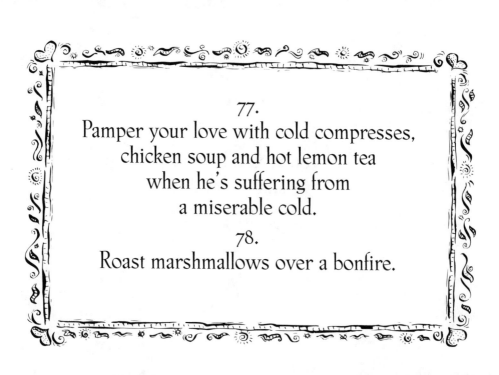

77.
Pamper your love with cold compresses,
chicken soup and hot lemon tea
when he's suffering from
a miserable cold.

78.
Roast marshmallows over a bonfire.

If you would be loved,
love and be lovable.

—BENJAMIN FRANKLIN

79.
Have a rock-skipping contest on
a misty afternoon.

80.
Share a childhood dream.

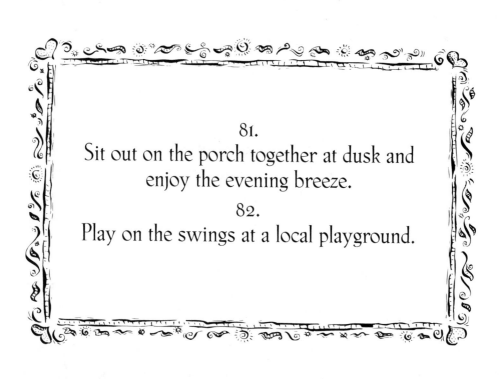

81.
Sit out on the porch together at dusk and enjoy the evening breeze.

82.
Play on the swings at a local playground.

There is more hunger
for love and appreciation in this world
than for bread.

—MOTHER THERESA

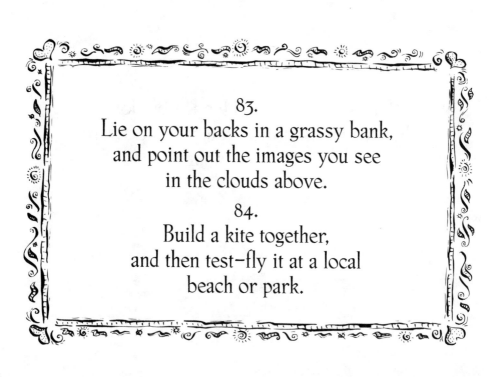

83.
Lie on your backs in a grassy bank,
and point out the images you see
in the clouds above.

84.
Build a kite together,
and then test-fly it at a local
beach or park.

When you have nothing left but love,
then for the first time you become aware
that love is enough.

—ANONYMOUS

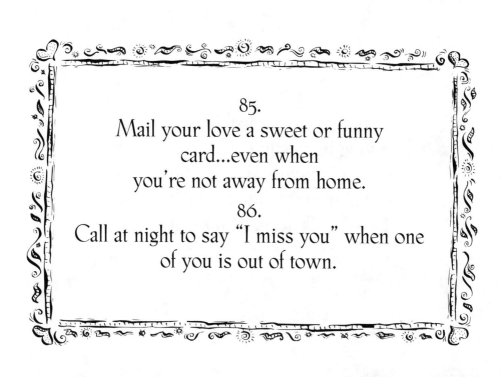

85.
Mail your love a sweet or funny
card...even when
you're not away from home.

86.
Call at night to say "I miss you" when one
of you is out of town.

Love alone is capable of uniting
living beings in such a way as to
complete and fulfill them,
for it alone takes them and joins them
by what is deepest in themselves.

—Pierre Teilhard de Chardin

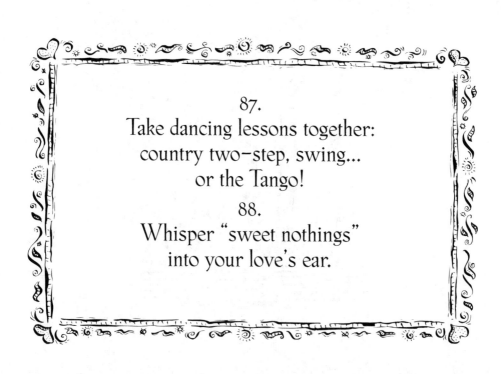

87.
Take dancing lessons together:
country two-step, swing...
or the Tango!

88.
Whisper "sweet nothings"
into your love's ear.

89.
Welcome your love home in a room
lit by candlelight.

90.
Give your total attention when your
love is speaking.

On this earth, though far and near,
without love, there's only fear.

—PEARL S. BUCK

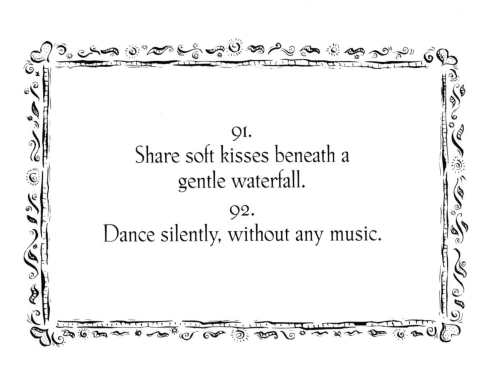

91.
Share soft kisses beneath a
gentle waterfall.

92.
Dance silently, without any music.

There isn't any formula or method.
You learn to love by loving.

—ALDOUS HUXLEY

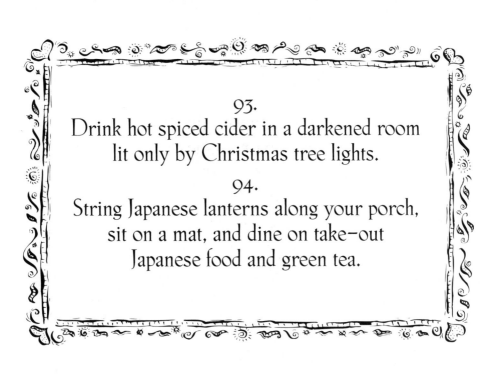

93.
Drink hot spiced cider in a darkened room lit only by Christmas tree lights.

94.
String Japanese lanterns along your porch, sit on a mat, and dine on take-out Japanese food and green tea.

Love lights more fire than
hate extinguishes.

—ELLA WHEELER WILCOX

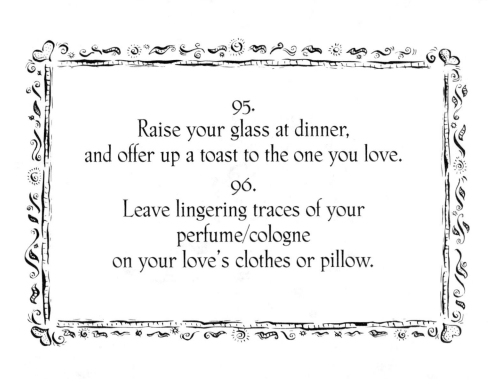

95.
Raise your glass at dinner,
and offer up a toast to the one you love.

96.
Leave lingering traces of your
perfume/cologne
on your love's clothes or pillow.

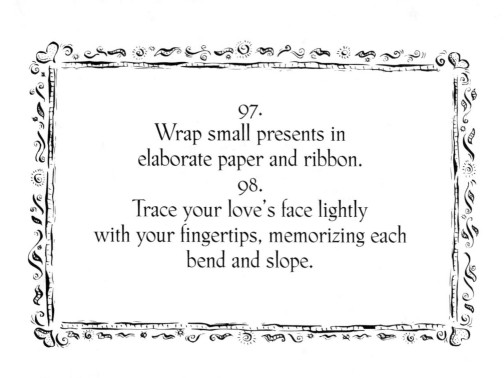

97.
Wrap small presents in
elaborate paper and ribbon.

98.
Trace your love's face lightly
with your fingertips, memorizing each
bend and slope.

However, each one of you also must love his wife as he loves himself, and the wife must respect her husband.

—EPHESIANS 5:33

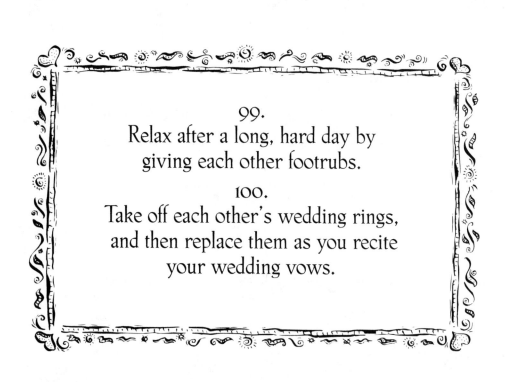

99.
Relax after a long, hard day by
giving each other footrubs.

100.
Take off each other's wedding rings,
and then replace them as you recite
your wedding vows.

Love doesn't just sit there, like a stone.
It has to be made like bread; remade all
the time, made new.

—Ursula K. Le Guin

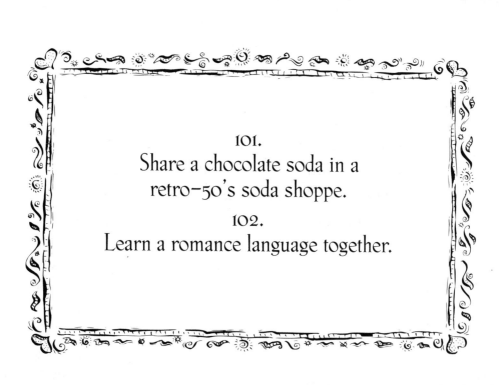

101.
Share a chocolate soda in a
retro-50's soda shoppe.

102.
Learn a romance language together.

There is the same difference in a person before and after he is in love, as there is in an unlighted lamp and one that is burning. The lamp was there and was a good lamp, but now it is shedding light too (and this is its real function).

—Vincent van Gogh

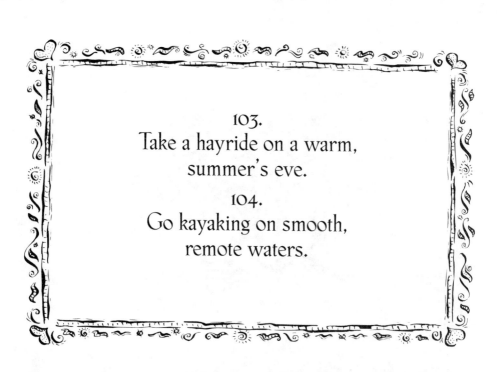

103.
Take a hayride on a warm,
summer's eve.

104.
Go kayaking on smooth,
remote waters.

105.
Visit an exotic island beach.

106.
Spend a romantic evening with your spouse at a secluded cabin, and go cross-country skiing together the next day.

If you're lucky, you'll get snowed in!

Is not this the true romantic feeling...
not to desire to escape life, but to
prevent life from escaping you?

—Thomas Clayton Wolfe

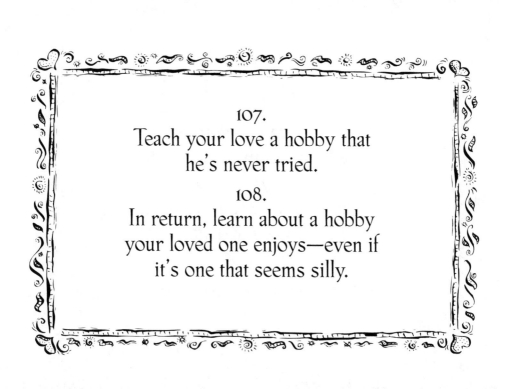

107.
Teach your love a hobby that
he's never tried.

108.
In return, learn about a hobby
your loved one enjoys—even if
it's one that seems silly.

Love grows by giving.
The love we give away is the
only love we keep.
The only way to retain love
is to give it away.

—ELBERT HUBBARD

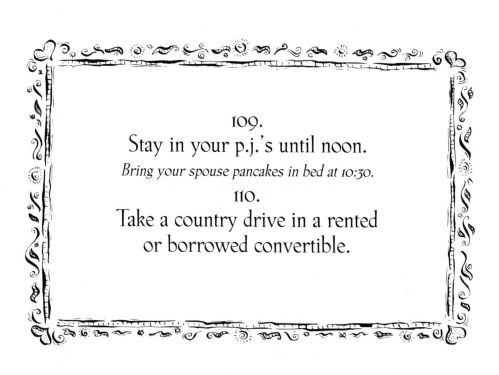

109.
Stay in your p.j.'s until noon.

Bring your spouse pancakes in bed at 10:30.

110.
Take a country drive in a rented
or borrowed convertible.

There is only one happiness in life:
to love and be loved.

—GEORGE SAND

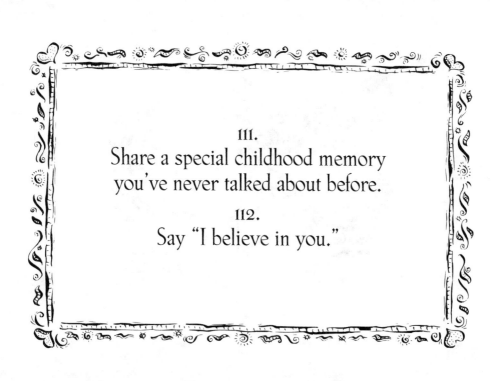

111.
Share a special childhood memory
you've never talked about before.

112.
Say "I believe in you."

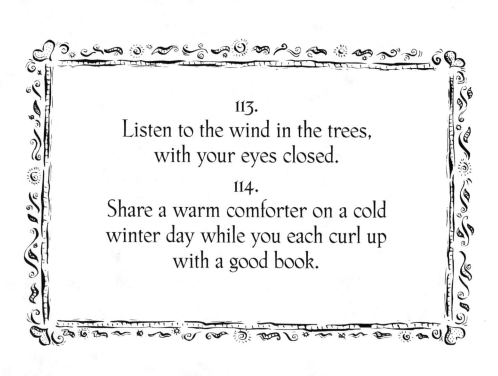

113.
Listen to the wind in the trees,
with your eyes closed.

114.
Share a warm comforter on a cold
winter day while you each curl up
with a good book.

I love thee with the breath,
Smiles, tears, of all my life!

—Elizabeth Barrett Browning

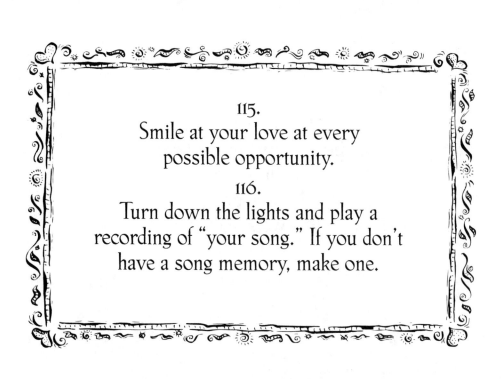

115.
Smile at your love at every
possible opportunity.

116.
Turn down the lights and play a
recording of "your song." If you don't
have a song memory, make one.

Freely we serve
Because we freely love,
as in our will
To love or not;
in this we stand or fall.

—JOHN MILTON

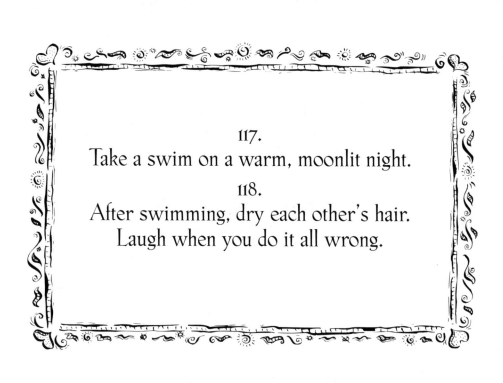

117.
Take a swim on a warm, moonlit night.

118.
After swimming, dry each other's hair.
Laugh when you do it all wrong.

Thus hand in hand
Through life we'll go
Through checkered paths
Of joy and woe.
We have loved on earth;
May we love in heaven.

—VERSE FROM A
NINETEENTH-CENTURY CARD

119.
Walk around the neighborhood
hand in hand after dinner.

120.
Adopt a homeless kitten or puppy
together from a local shelter.

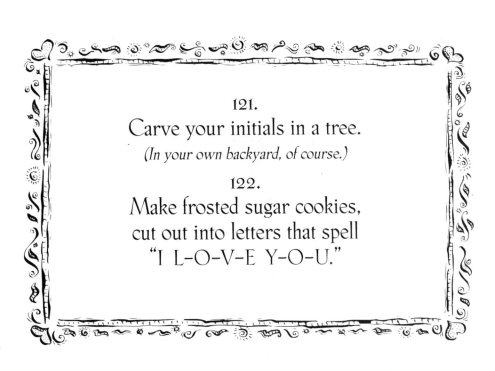

121.
Carve your initials in a tree.
(In your own backyard, of course.)

122.
Make frosted sugar cookies,
cut out into letters that spell
"I L–O–V–E Y–O–U."

Love is not a feeling but a choice.

—Soren Kierkegaard

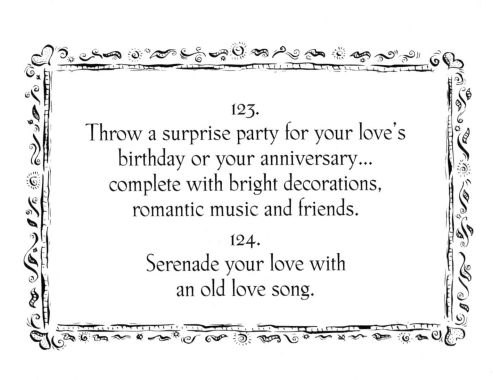

123.
Throw a surprise party for your love's
birthday or your anniversary...
complete with bright decorations,
romantic music and friends.

124.
Serenade your love with
an old love song.

How do I love thee?
Let me count the ways.

—Elizabeth Barrett Browning

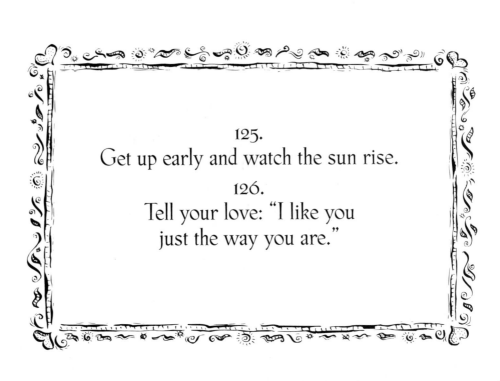

125.
Get up early and watch the sun rise.

126.
Tell your love: "I like you
just the way you are."

O love is the crooked thing,
There is nobody wise enough
To find out all that is in it,
For he would be thinking of love
Till the stars had run away
And the shadows eaten the moon...

—WILLIAM BUTLER YEATS

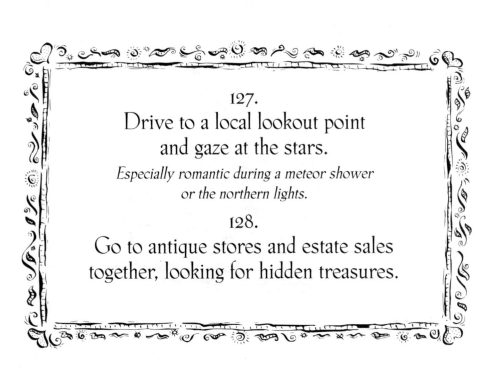

127.
Drive to a local lookout point
and gaze at the stars.
*Especially romantic during a meteor shower
or the northern lights.*

128.
Go to antique stores and estate sales
together, looking for hidden treasures.

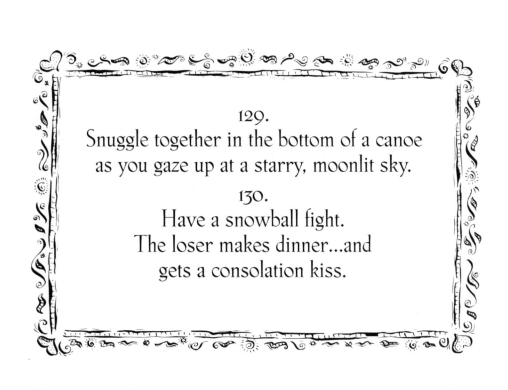

129.
Snuggle together in the bottom of a canoe
as you gaze up at a starry, moonlit sky.

130.
Have a snowball fight.
The loser makes dinner...and
gets a consolation kiss.

It is not our toughness that keeps us
warm at night, but our tenderness which
makes others want to keep us warm.

—HAROLD LYON

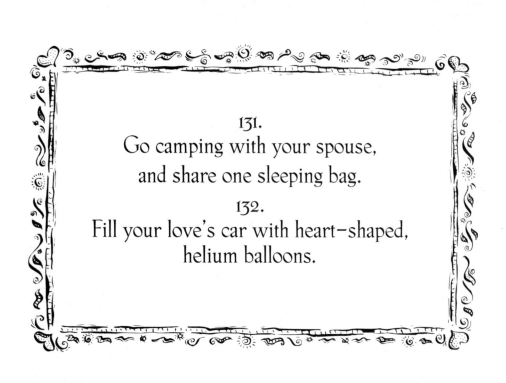

131.
Go camping with your spouse,
and share one sleeping bag.

132.
Fill your love's car with heart-shaped,
helium balloons.

That thou didst know how many
fathom deep I am in love!

—SHAKESPEARE

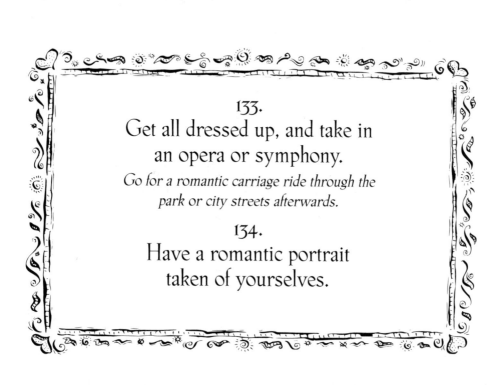

133.
Get all dressed up, and take in
an opera or symphony.
*Go for a romantic carriage ride through the
park or city streets afterwards.*

134.
Have a romantic portrait
taken of yourselves.

Marriage must exemplify friendship's highest ideal, or else it will be a failure.

—MARGARET E. SANGSTER, 1904

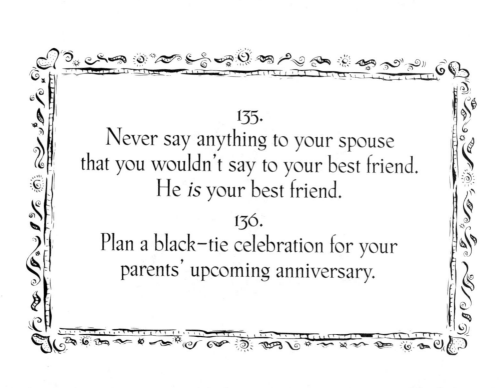

135.
Never say anything to your spouse
that you wouldn't say to your best friend.
He *is* your best friend.

136.
Plan a black-tie celebration for your
parents' upcoming anniversary.

137.
Build two snow people...that look like the two of you!

138.
When you wake up, talk about what you dreamed.

Love comforteth like sunshine after rain.

—WILLIAM SHAKESPEARE

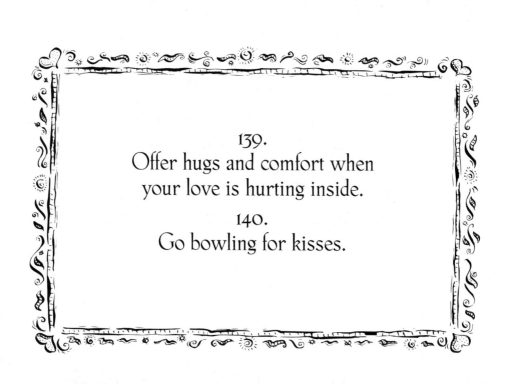

139.
Offer hugs and comfort when
your love is hurting inside.

140.
Go bowling for kisses.

If the king had given me Paris,
his great city, and if Iwere required
to give up my darling love, I would
say to King Henry: 'Take your Paris
back; I prefer my darling, by the ford,
I prefer my darling.'

—ANONYMOUS

141.
Send flowers to your love at work...
so *everyone* can see how much you care.

142.
Pack a warm blanket and cuddle up
at a drive-in movie.

Let those love now,
who never lov'd before:
Let those who always lov'd,
now love the more.

—ANONYMOUS

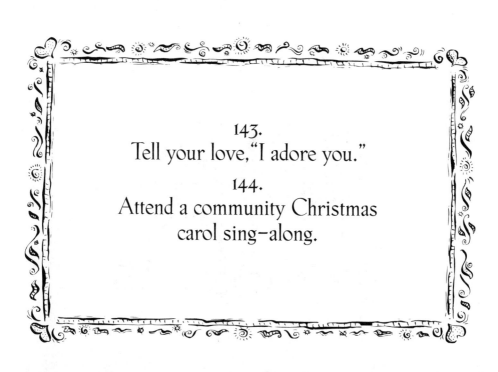

143.
Tell your love, "I adore you."

144.
Attend a community Christmas carol sing-along.

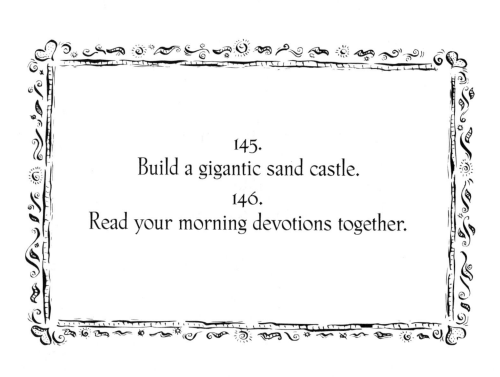

145.
Build a gigantic sand castle.

146.
Read your morning devotions together.

But the fruit of the Spirit is love,
joy, peace, patience, kindness,
goodness, faithfulness, gentleness
and self-control.

—GALATIANS 5:22

147.
Learn to say "I'm sorry."

148.
Forgive...forgive...forgive.
Nothing impedes romance
like hard feelings.

I knew it was love, and
I felt it was glory.

—LORD BYRON

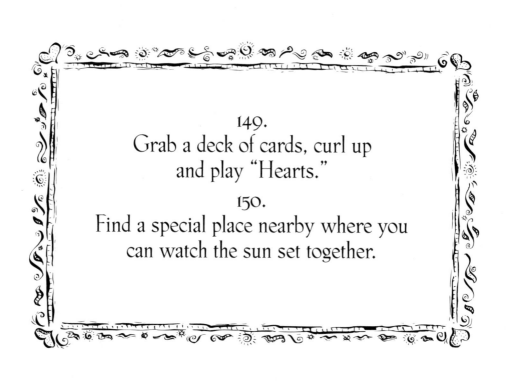

149.
Grab a deck of cards, curl up
and play "Hearts."

150.
Find a special place nearby where you
can watch the sun set together.

About the Author

A graduate of the University of California, Irvine,
Lisa Tawn Bergren holds a bachelor of arts in English Literature.
She has implemented at least 75 of the 150 suggestions
in *Romantic Notions*, and looks forward to the next 75
(as does her husband).

If you enjoyed these *Romantic Notions*, you'll want
to read *Refuge*, a contemporary Christian romance
also by Lisa Tawn Bergren.

In Montana's Breathtaking
Elk Horn Valley, They Found Adventure,
Love...and Life.

Witness the struggles and hope of two couples drawn
together by God's mighty plan in *Refuge*.